THE

FIRST

FLAME

A Prequel to The Last Suttee

MADHU BAZAZ WANGU

Copyright © 2023 Madhu Bazaz Wangu
All Rights Reserved

 Year of the Book
135 Glen Avenue
Glen Rock, PA 17327

No part of this publication may be reproduced, distributed, or transmitted in any form or by any means, including photocopying, recording, or other electronic or mechanical methods, without the prior written permission of the publisher, except in the case of brief quotations embodied in critical reviews and certain other noncommercial uses permitted by copyright law.

This book is a work of fiction. Names, characters, places, and incidents are products of the author's imagination or are used fictitiously. Any resemblance to actual events or locations or persons, living or dead, is entirely coincidental.

ISBN: 978-1-64649-363-0 (paperback)
ISBN: 978-1-64649-364-7 (ebook)

OTHER BOOKS

Fiction

The Last Suttee

The Other Shore

The Immigrant Wife

Chance Meetings

Non-Fiction

Unblock Your Creative Flow

Images of Indian Goddesses

A Goddess is Born

Hinduism

Buddhism

CDs

Mindful Meditation for Writers: Body, Heart, Mind

Mindful Meditation for Writers II: Walking Through the Forest, Awakening the Senses, Mountain and Lotus, Animating Seven Energy Chakra

Meditations for Mindful Writers III: Generosity, Gratitude, Self-Compassion and Trust

Kumud Kuthiyala could not hide her excitement at the thought of Saubhagya Massi's visit on Diwali Eve, the festival of lights. Sau Massi was her honorary aunt and her mother's best friend. Since that morning at the beginning of her school's weeklong vacation, Kumud had been Ma's cooking assistant and helped ready Sau's room. Now they were making cotton wicks for *diyas* to be lit on Diwali Eve.

To avoid accidental burns, Kumud's mother Geeta knotted her own long silken hair into a low bun, and instead of wearing a sari, she donned a churidar and shirt. She had also left her long scarf on the back of a kitchen chair.

After Kumud placed the final wick in its earthenware lamp, Ma carefully filled them all halfway with sesame oil. The *diyas* would be lit and burn as long as the oil lasted.

Ma loaded one tray with lamps and was about to carry it when Kumud said, "Ma, I can take these."

"Are you sure?"

"I'm ten, Ma. Let me do this."

"Not yet," Ma replied. After tying Kumud's two braids in a knot behind her back, Ma's beautiful black eyes shined with pride. "Okay take it, but be careful, *bitiya rani!* These thirteen *diyas* are for the puja room upstairs. Arrange them on the windowsill so they are visible from afar."

"Tell me again, why *thirteen*?"

"Today is the thirteenth day of the lunar fortnight, *Triyodashi,* one of the three auspicious days of Diwali," Ma answered. "On this day Lord Shiva bestows long life, peace, and good fortune, and Laxmi, the goddess of prosperity, visits us."

Kumud gingerly picked up the tray and was about to leave when her mother repeated, "Be careful! Should I come with you?"

"No Ma, I can do this!"

After a few minutes, Kumud returned triumphmant. "Where do I go next?"

"You're back already. Good girl!" Together they arranged lamps on the windowsills and the front porch. Out of the blue Ma said, "Let's light them before your father and Sau arrive."

"But the sun hasn't set yet."

"It will be dark when they get here. Besides, that will leave us more time to sit with Sau before dinner." Ma struck a matchstick and used it to light two candles. She handed one taper to Kumud and kept one for herself. "Go, big girl. Light the ones in the courtyard and I will do the rest. Be careful!"

"You keep saying that."

"We have to be extra attentive. Lamps are beautiful but they can also burn. Remember behind their beauty they hide danger."

Kumud nodded with understanding. Ma's words gave her a pause. "Our teacher taught us about fire. She said it helps cook food, provides warmth, but it can also destroy and cause pain."

"Exactly," Ma agreed. "Did you learn how on the day of Diwali, light represents removal of darkness the way knowledge removes ignorance?"

Kumud thought for a moment. "I like that lesson."

"These are good teachings. You already know about Agni, the god of fire, and Laxmi, the goddess who blesses people on the night of Diwali, don't you?"

Kumud gave her mother a big grin. "We light lamps to welcome the gods and goddesses to our home."

"Exactly. Now go and help remove darkness." Ma straightened the candle Kumud was holding and looked at her face. "It's nice to see you smiling so much. I'm glad you're excited."

"I'm so happy Sau Massi is coming."

"She adores you." Ma patted Kumud's head. "Let's finish lighting the lamps. They are soon to arrive."

Under the moonless indigo sky, in the darkest night of the lunar month, row after shimmering row of thousands of *diyas* on windowsills and porches illuminated the neighborhood. The nightscape looked like fairies emerging from darkness.

From the kitchen window Kumud heard the sound of her father's motorbike. Her heart was bursting with joy. She ran to the front porch followed by her mother.

On his motorbike, Baba was the talk of the town because he was the only one who owned such a vehicle. A couple of the elders of Sau's city of Neela Nagar owned cars, but the novelty of a two-wheeler excited the townspeople. They watched him speed by wearing headgear, his tie flying like the hero of a Bollywood movie. And now here he was bringing Kumud's favorite person from the bus depot to their home. This was the best day ever!

Mother and daughter greeted their guest as if they had not seen each other in ages. They hugged, they kissed, they laughed.

"Don't feel left out, Raguji. We love you too!" Sau Massi kidded Kumud's father.

"I'm enjoying watching you ladies," he said good-naturedly. He carried Sau's duffle and handbag to the guest room.

The women had settled on chairs around the table in the courtyard when Baba returned. "Geeta, do you have the *mithai* plates ready for the neighbors?" he asked. "Kumud and I can deliver them. I don't want to have to go out after dinner."

"They are ready on the kitchen counter. While you two go, I'll get dinner started. Oh, but don't take the *mithai* plates we received from the neighbors."

"That would be embarrassing. Which ones then?"

"Take the ones covered with doilies," she told him.

"I can help," Sau Massi said.

"No, you go wash up," Ma encouraged. "You must be tired. I'll make a hot cup of tea for you."

"That sounds good!" Sau said and she went to the room where Ragu had carried her baggage.

Geeta was putting dinner on the table in the dining room, adjacent to the kitchen, when everyone returned. But before dining, it was time for Kumud's favorite part of the festival of lights. Families competed without saying a word. A battle of fireworks was repeated every year on the eve of Diwali. For a better view, some elderly people watched from their porches or the second-story windows of their homes.

At twilight, girls and their mothers made shapes in the air with sparklers. Younger boys daringly fired rows of crackers, making a racket. And as soon as the sky turned dark, the Gupta and Aggarwal families—who boasted about their teenage boys—got ready with heaps of fountains, wheels, and rockets, more to show off than to entertain.

The Gupta father and son duo started with the wheels, two at a time whirling on the ground, shooting sparkling lines and dots. The Aggarwals joined them, lighting one fountain at a time, which made similar shiny lines and stars that first shot up and then curved downward. Before the gunpowder of one firecracker was consumed, the next one was lit, so that the air was never without a glittering show.

Kumud, along with other boys and girls, watched while holding her sparkler, shouting with joy while also keeping an eye on the neighbors to see who had the better fireworks.

During a pause, Baba lit two fountains at once. One shot higher than the other. It was the highest of all the fountains so far, making the spectators clap and hoot. Baba had only bought them because they were Kumud and Ma's favorite. He lit the rest one by one, to the joy of everyone, until they were done.

Now it was time for the rockets. These seemed to be favorites of the Aggarwal family. Each pierced the dark sky, though some only shot a couple of stories high and then looped down to the ground. Perhaps the rocket was not of good quality, or its chemical reaction with the powder was not enough. They just went *fuusss,* striking against the wall or a row of trees.

One by one the heap of fireworks depleted, but each family had saved some for the finale. A neighbor announced it was time for the spectacular climax. At once, the remaining wheels, fountains, rockets, and snappers were lit... and within moments the finale was over. Whether a family had lit five or fifty fireworks, each enjoyed the grand *tamasha* and was a bit sad for it to end. Only clouds of smoke remained visible against the dark sky.

Kumud heard giggles and laughs until that too quieted down as people hurried back to their homes to enjoy the festive dinner. The grand show had helped build everyone's appetite.

With Baba at the head of the table and Ma at his left, Kumud sat to his right next to Sau Massi. Dishes were passed around—corn *roti, Ram pulao, aloo kulcha, brinjal sabzi,* a flavorful concoction of *brinjal* and potatoes, and *moong dal.*

After tasting a spoonful of *brinjal* Sau said, "Thanks for making this, Geeta. It's so good."

"Kumud helped me," Geeta replied. "That's why everything tastes yummier." She pushed the dish toward Sau. "I know how you love it."

Sau turned to Kumud. "You have grown so much since I saw you last. How long has it been?"

"Almost one year!" Kumud jumped with the answer.

After the meal, the ladies cleared the table and Baba prepared tea to serve with the *mithai* sweetmeats. They talked about old friends from Neela Nagar, Sau Massi's grown children, and finally Sau's husband who'd been ill, but had remained stable for over a month. That was the reason Sau was able to visit. Her husband had insisted that she needed respite, and her stepsons offered to help him while she was gone.

Until recently it had been torturous for Saubhagya. She herself had begun to experience bouts of exhaustion and pain. As she told them about her situation, they grew silent and sad, but Sau turned to Kumud, changing the subject. "On this Deepavali day, what do you wish for the Laxmi to bless you with?"

"Can she get my homework done?" Kumud asked, lightening the mood.

Sau Massi laughed with a mischievous twinkle in her eyes.

"That would be more like a curse," Ma interjected. "Instead of lighting your mind with knowledge she would be keeping it dark."

"We learned in school that Laxmi is the goddess of money."

"That she is, *bitiya*!" Baba affirmed. "But do you know what the collective glow of *diyas* means?"

"Light in darkness," Kumud replied automatically. "And Ma said they represent knowledge that replaces ignorance."

"Great answer!" Ma beamed.

"Also the little lamps represent the triumph of light over darkness, good over evil," Baba continued. "While we sleep, people believe that Laxmi walks through our homes to ward off negative energy and evil spirits, leaving behind well-being, health and prosperity."

"You think she will come to our home, Baba?"

"If she visits everyone, she will certainly visit us," he assured.

"Time to go to bed, *bitiya*," her mother announced.

"I'm not sleepy. I want to sit with Sau Massi a little longer." Kumud put her head on Sau's shoulder.

"It's almost midnight," Ma reminded. "Sau will be with us for the whole week."

"You do look tired!" Sau said, caressing Kumud's hair. "We are going to have plenty of fun this week."

Kumud slept well. In the morning when she entered the kitchen, she found her mother and Sau Massi making *puris*, deep fried puffed bread. From a mound of dough on a plate, Sau shaped a handful between the palms of her hands, then rolled it out and placed it in the *kadayi*, a kind of wok, half-full of smoking oil.

Using a sieve, Ma gently pressed a couple of *puris* against the pan's surface and then flipped them to fry the other side. She let each drain over the wok for a few seconds then stacked them on a plate covered with newspaper to let the oil drain. A bowl of sweet semolina *halwa* sprinkled with slivered almonds and raisins was also waiting to be consumed.

The aroma made Kumud's mouth water. It was amazing how only a minute or two turned the dough to luscious golden brown.

"Namaste, Sau Massi and Ma. Can I make a *puri*?" she asked.

"Namaste, Kumud. Of course!" Sau moved to the side, making space for Kumud to step into the assembly line.

Ma gave her a one-arm hug and went back to frying.

Steam from the flavorful sugary tea must have floated through the house because Kumud's father walked in with his morning paper. "After last night's dinner, I thought I wouldn't ever be hungry again. Yet here I am, ready to eat the aromatic breakfast you ladies have prepared." He took a seat in the kitchen. "Come sit with me, *bitiya!*"

"Just a minute, Baba. I'm helping." Kumud turned to her mother. "Can I roll and fry a *puri* for Baba?"

"Yes, you may." Ma guided her to roll and gently slide the *puri* into the hot oil.

Excited by the outcome of her first attempt Kumud said, "I want to make another one for you and one for Sau Massi."

Soon the *puri, halwa* and tea were served. All relished each morsel, nodding their heads and complimenting the youngest cook with encouraging remarks.

Feeling good about her cooking debut Kumud said, "What are we going to do today?" to no one in particular. She wrapped a morsel of *halwa* in a piece of *puri* and waited.

The crack of random fireworks interrupted their conversation.

"Did you hear that?" Baba remarked. "Some neighbors apparently didn't finish their pile last night and are too impatient to wait until dark. *Bevkoof*, idiots!"

"We will take Sau Massi to Diwali Mela and wherever else she wants to go," Ma finally responded to Kumud's question. "But first we must collect all the *diyas*, and I need to cook a few dishes in advance, since we will be out most of the next couple of days."

"Kumud, let's get the *diyas* from the front porch and the windowsills on this floor," Sau said. "Then you can help me clean them while Geeta cooks."

"Clean the *diyas*?" Kumud asked. "Why? Usually, Ma just drains out the oil and wipes them."

"I'll show you how to get rid of the layer of grease so they look almost new."

Ma got busy in the kitchen while Sau Massi and Kumud collected the stacks of *diyas*.

Baba asked Sau, "What do you clean them with?"

"That concoction." Sau pointed to a plastic bucket near the water faucet. "A mixture of salt and vinegar in warm water. We'll soak the lamps for half an hour or so, scrub the interior, and then dip them in clean water.

Then we'll rub them clean with newspaper scraps and lay them out to dry in the sunlight."

"A long process, isn't it?"

"But it removes the oily stains and gets rid of the smell."

Kumud went to fetch the rest of the *diyas* while Baba sat reading the paper. Ma continued her cooking and Sau Massi was already dipping the lamps in the bucket when another blast of fireworks crackled.

"Did you hear that?" Ma called out. "Why can't they wait until it gets dark and the whole neighborhood could enjoy what they're burning away now!"

Suddenly, Kumud shrieked. Something had hit her on the side of her face. She cried out in pain and fell to the ground.

Rocking back and forth, she cried for Ma. It felt as if someone had sprinkled red chili powder on the side of her face.

Sau ran upstairs and Ma followed. The two women gasped in shock. Kumud's right hand cupped her right cheek and ear. She writhed in pain, crying.

As soon as Geeta saw the child she ran back to the kitchen.

Sau sat on the floor next to Kumud. "Oh my goodness!"

Baba arrived now as well. "A firecracker hit you, didn't it?" he said rubbing her back.

"It hurts, Baba... badly."

In minutes Ma returned holding a bowl in one hand, stirring it with the index finger of the other.

"Quick thinking, Geeta!" Baba said.

"What's that?" Kumud asked.

"A mixture of turmeric powder, mustard oil and acacia extract. So sorry, *bitiya*. I knew someone was going to get hurt. So unsafe."

"Who lights fireworks during the daytime?" Baba remarked. "Bunch of *bevkoofs*!"

"Is it going to hurt?" Kumud asked.

"No, *bitiya*. It's a cooling potion," Ma said. "It will reduce your pain."

Kumud leaned against Sau's bosom, and her mother sat next to her, tenderly dabbing the paste against her cheek and the edge of her ear.

Sau Massi gently blew on the burned area to make it feel cooler.

"It stings!" Kumud squealed.

"Just the first time," Ma said. "It will get better with each application."

"How many times do you need to put it on?"

"A few. Perhaps every ten to fifteen minutes."

To make her feel better Sau added, "It isn't as bad as I thought, Kumud. This paste will also clear the skin, so it won't leave any marks."

Kumud's mother kissed her hand. "I should have closed the window last night and collected the *diyas* myself."

"Don't blame yourself, Geeta," Baba said. "It was an accident which could have been avoided if certain *bevkoofs* had some sense."

For a moment the room was quiet.

Kumud moaned when Sau gently re-applied the paste over her wounds.

Ma turned to Baba, her voice tense. "Should we go to a doctor?"

"I examined the wound," Baba said. "It is more of a shock than a deep burn."

"Good that you quickly prepared the paste," Sau said to Ma, then patted Kumud's shoulder. "In a few days you'll be okay."

"I feel terrible," Ma said guiltily.

"Accidents happen, Geeta. She will be fine."

Ma offered her hand to help Kumud get up. "Let's go to your room. You can rest for a while until the pain subsides."

Kumud wiped her eyes. "I didn't think fire could hurt so much."

When she woke, the house was quiet. Kumud walked to the kitchen and noticed that the plastic bucket was turned upside down. Next to it stood columns of *diyas* ready to be taken outside under the sun. Ma and Sau Massi were happily chatting over cups of tea.

Kumud picked up a *diya*. "Look Ma, they shine like new! We can use them next year!"

"Has the pain gone?" Sau Massi asked grinning.

"It feels better," Kumud agreed.

Her mother prompted, "Take a seat. Time for more turmeric paste."

The next morning Kumud's cheek and ear only tingled. Ma applied another round of turmeric paste before they left for the famous local fair, the annual Diwali Mela. The trip could no longer be postponed as it was the last of three days of festivities.

Sau Massi consoled, "I promise that before I leave, your face will look as beautiful as when I arrived."

It was late afternoon when the three ladies, all dressed up, left home. Her father never accompanied them to the mela, so they didn't force him. The bus drove them as close as possible and then dropped them where the road ended and the vast sandy area began.

There were still several hours until sunset. When they got closer to the arena, Kumud could see booths and kiosks of trinkets and bangles, and hear singing voices and the playing of drums and harmoniums. Then came the cacophony of camels decked in full regalia. The elaborate coverings on their backs had been intricately embroidered in reds, greens, yellows and blues, and were studded with mirrors that reflected light. Their owners, sporting full beards and mustaches, were dressed in white, walking their camels or chatting in groups of two or three.

The three ladies walked under the entrance sign that glittered, "Welcome to Diwali Mela!"

Just inside the gate, a group of six men on camels brandished their swords, engaging in mock battle to amuse the spectators. Adjacent stood a group of boys with smaller swords, dancing with rhythmic fencing motions to the accompaniment of a drum. On the opposite side were women wearing black robes sewn with glowing mirrors and bead work. Their flouncy skirts and long transparent scarves whirled as their feet pirouetted. These women balanced three brass pots of diminishing sizes over their heads. Ma, Sau Massi and Kumud stood mesmerized with their acrobatic skill.

The wide but straight pathway was flanked by booths of different sizes on the way to the arena at the distant end. Smaller kiosks stood on wooden platforms. Kumud ogled the colorful wares—decorative lanterns, hand purses, and shoulder bags made out of leather and jute, as well as bangles of rainbow colors, odni-scarves, and fancy kitchen gadgets.

Then the large open-air theater booths came into view. Various singing, dancing and gaming shows were being performed directly on the sandy ground. The performers played string or wind instruments, beat on drums, or sang accompanied by harmonium —a reed organ that has a keyboard like a piano.

A woman danced with castanets made from rosewood with bells attached. Accompanied by the rhythm of a drum and a folk singer, she danced her heart out, ignoring the blaring Bollywood songs from a loudspeaker elsewhere.

A big banner on one booth read, "Who Wants to Be Mr. Desert?" A row of men on the stage faced the spectators in this contest for the most impressive mustache and beard. A man's mustache was considered to be a symbol of brawn and bravery.

Some individuals from the audience were also invited to join the competition. They were individually inspected then either accepted or rejected. Only the finalists joined the ones standing in a row on stage.

The time of selection was just minutes away. Some men nervously touched the hair over their upper lip and chin, making sure it was still there. Finally, a man who claimed a foot-long mustache was asked to untwirl it for measurement. A judge brandishing a wooden ruler confirmed the boast as the man untwirled the five circles of his enormous mustache. Only then did the audience clap for supposedly the most valorous man in town. Or at least the most valorous for that year.

Adjacent to "Mr. Desert," the "Miss Desert" competition was underway. This title was awarded to the woman wearing the most gorgeous bridal attire, including jewelry and footwear. This time no one from the audience was invited. Each participant was gorgeous. To Kumud, each one looked like a winner.

The three ladies decided to move on to the next booth where a turban tying competition was in full swing. The local style of *pagdi* used thirty-some feet of material folded in a specialized manner. It required special skill and was so complicated that wearing a *pagdi* was a sign worthy of respect.

The next booth was crowded so Kumud stepped aside for Ma and Sau Massi to get a closer and better look. The women found them a spot and the show turned out to be a snake charmer playing *pungi*. The flute sounds enticed and hypnotized the cobra, making him sway gracefully.

A vibrantly dressed female dancer in red and glittering stripes of silver appeared from nowhere. She made gestures similar to the movement of the snake in rhythm with the *pungi*. Her outfit shimmered under the setting sun and *gungurus*—dancing bells tied from her ankles up to her knees—jingled as she imitated the cobra's swaying. She held cymbals in her hands and played them in time with the movement of her legs. The *pungi* and *gungurus* had a bewitching effect and the audience sat spellbound.

Kumud, Sau Massi and Ma made a stop at a knickknack kiosk. Kumud examined all sorts of bangles—glass, lacquer, silver and brass. She asked Ma if she could buy some. Her mother nodded. Each got busy looking at a variety of items hanging from wooden poles and different sides of the rectangular cart.

Kumud selected some and then a jute purse.

"Who is that for?" Geeta asked.

"I'll pay for it from my pocket money."

"That's not what I asked."

"For Sau Massi," Kumud whispered.

At one end of the cart hung exquisitely designed lanterns, hand painted and inlaid. Geeta couldn't resist buying two, one for their home and one for their dear guest.

The same cart offered *diyas* which were as beautifully made as the lanterns. "Can we buy *diyas* for next year, Ma?"

"We have perfectly fine *diyas*, thanks to Sau Massi. Why buy more?"

"But these are beautiful like brides. Ours look like beggars."

Ma and Sau Massi laughed.

"Please Ma, just thirteen." She chose a number she knew her mother considered auspicious.

"Please let me buy these for Kumud, Geeta," Sau Massi said so earnestly that Geeta could not refuse.

The sun soon set. The moonless sky was now turning dark. In the main arena the show was about to start, one not to be missed. The three women hurried down the pathway.

Men had prepared a four-by-eight-foot bed of coal using soft wood burnt down end to end. Now glowing embers, tiny blue flames, flickered from the ash-covered pieces of coal.

As soon as Kumud reached the rope that separated the performers from the spectators a suppressed cry tore from her mouth. "Maaaa!" She cupped the part of her face that had burned the day before.

Sau Massi put a hand around her shoulders. "What's wrong? Are you okay?"

"The flames remind me of my burn."

"We don't have to watch this," her mother said.

"What are they going to do on that burning coal?" Kumud asked.

"The firewalkers will walk on them to show how strong they are—that fire can't burn them."

"Why would they do that? Surely they'll get hurt." Kumud sounded panicked.

"This charcoal is not as hot as that firecracker that burned you," Sau Massi consoled. "Besides, they have practiced walking on burning coal for years. And see how the coals are thinly coated with ash."

"The soles of our feet are not as sensitive as our faces," Ma added. "Plus these men walk briskly. The time of contact with the hot coals is minimal. You'll see how they emerge unscathed. Don't worry."

Ma and Sau Massi explained all they could to alleviate Kumud's anxiety, but she could not stop thinking about the fear and pain of her recent burns. She gazed at the coal pieces covered with ash, tiny bluish flames jutting out of the cracks. Shiny sparks emerged and disappeared into the dark.

The women asked Kumud to step away from the heat. A drum rolled. The three of them turned and walked to the fence line.

People clapped and shouted, "Go! Go! Go!"

As Kumud watched the men step on the bed of coal she felt a mild sensation of burning on her own feet. But the whole show lasted only for minutes. And then it was over. After all the anxiety Kumud had suffered, it was an anticlimactic ending.

Quickly her ears perked at an announcement coming from the loudspeaker. Her favorite *kathputli* show—a string marionette dance-drama—was about to begin. She smiled and asked Ma and Sau Massi to walk faster as she herself strode toward the theater booth she had noticed earlier.

The production of marionette dolls, carved from wood and dressed in colorful folk finery, was a favorite of almost all the mela goers. Kumud wondered which story they would enact that evening.

They arrived just as the show started and sat on the floor in front of a makeshift stage.

A man playing the harmonium made an announcement. "Being the last evening of the Mela, we will perform not just one, but *two shows!*"

Kumud couldn't hide her excitement, all painful thoughts of the firewalkers now vanished.

"The first is the tale of the fourteenth-century queen Rani Padmavati, the most beautiful queen of Chittor," the announcer continued. "And the second will be that of Devi Narayani."

Kathputli dance-drama was the ultimate entertainment. Kumud sat riveted as puppets enacted Queen Rani Padmavati's tragic story. A man sang folk lyrics accompanied by a drum and harmonium. When King Ratan Singh's puppet character was defeated and killed in the war for the Fort of Chittorgarh, Kumud sat spellbound watching as news reached the puppet queen. Padmavati and fourteen other women jumped into the funeral pyre with their king, committing ritual suttee to save their honor.

After walking and standing the whole day, the ladies now felt hungry. During intermission, Kumud fetched packets of roasted spicy chickpeas, chat-masala and cold cola while Ma and Sau Massi saved her seat. Soon the next half of the show began.

The second story was about how an ordinary girl became a goddess in her lifetime. A couple, Ganga and Govinda, were unable to have a child. After years of prayer and alms giving, they had a baby girl named Narayani. One night Ganga dreamed that Narayani was the great goddess herself, incarnated as their daughter.

Kumud once more sat entranced as puppet Narayani impressed her teachers by memorizing *Vedas, Bhagavad Gita,* and *Ramayana,* Hindu scriptures and epics, before she was even ten years old. Impressed with her understanding of scriptures and dedication to learning, her father taught her fencing, shooting, and horseback riding at home.

When Narayani turned thirteen, her parents began to search for a suitable boy and found Tanmandas. Narayani's father gave a dowry, including three-wheeled *chakdas* and a white mare, Tanmandas's favorite.

Kumud watched as the newly married puppet couple—riding in their three-wheel buggy pulled by the impressive mare—was accosted by a jealous man who lured Tanmandas from the vehicle, killed him, and took the prized horse.

Puppet Narayani witnessed the murder of her beloved husband, and with the smoky fumes of her anger she transformed into the battle goddess Kali, who asked the guard to take her husband's bloodied body to a designated place.

She first slew her husband's murderer, then returned to the place where she was to meet her guard. He had collected firewood for the cremation. Narayani declared that she had decided to commit suttee. She joined her husband on the firewood, taking his head in her lap.

The guard stood with his palms together as he saw the manifestation of the great goddess in Narayani.

Tears poured from Kumud's eyes, and those of other audience members, as puppet Narayani covered her head and face with the *pallu* of her sari. The mound was lit and its flames touched the sky. Then a melodious voice from the mound said, *"Pour water!"* The other puppets doused the mound with water and the fire was extinguished.

When the show ended, no one moved. A silence held the audience in place like a spell. Then after half a minute, everyone cheered wildly before rising to leave.

The hectic day and heat had exhausted Kumud. Plus the show made her think. With shoulders slouched, she walked ahead of her mother and Sau Massi toward the exit.

She heard Ma and Sau arguing. No other topic made them squabble as much as suttee. Kumud hastened her pace. She hated when the two women she loved most dearly did not agree. Even though their anger usually fizzled quickly, at that moment Kumud wished only to disconnect from their heated argument.

Her muscles tightened. The skin of her face tingled with suppressed discomfort. Something was not right. What was it that made Kumud feel emotionally exposed? A strange kind of restlessness settled in her heart.

Once home, Kumud's mood changed. Her father had lovingly set a full meal for them. Men usually didn't help in the kitchen but Baba was different, and Ma obligingly thanked him.

"Ragu, why didn't you serve the extra dishes we prepared yesterday?" Sau Massi asked with a hint of guilt.

Baba was in a jovial mood. "I wanted to surprise you, Sau," he responded.

Kumud wondered how her father's cooking would taste.

When each had something nice to say to Baba, a smile played on his lips. "I can clean up," he said kindly. "You ladies take it easy."

Kumud saw her mother wink at her. She didn't know why.

"I'm not tired from cooking," he sighed. "I just heated the dishes. I got everything from *Homelike Khana Halwai* shop." Then he laughed.

"I knew," Ma said.

"Then why didn't you say something?" he asked.

"I didn't want to spoil your surprise." Ma laughed as did everyone else.

Sau Massi was the one fooled the most. "You are a practical joker, aren't you?"

Once in bed, Kumud was too tired to fall asleep. Her vacation days were passing by fast. She was already starting to miss her favorite aunt. But Ma had promised they would visit Sau Massi's home in a few months. The thought soothed her somewhat.

Kumud reminded herself what Sau always said. *"Don't be sad. Think of the next time we are going to be together. Something to look forward to, right?"* Then they would hug. And so that's what Kumud decided to do—she thought of seeing Sau Massi at her home in just a few months. Before she knew it, she was fast asleep.

After Sau left to visit the local Satimata temple with Mrs. Aggarwal the following morning, Kumud asked her mother, "Why didn't we go to the temple with Sau Massi?"

"Because we're not Satimata devotees. We don't believe in suttee." Then pointing to the seat next to her, Ma said, "Come sit here with me. I want to have a special mother-daughter talk with you."

"About what?"

"As you know, Sau Massi feels differently about Satimata than I do. She is her devotee. She believes in the ritual of suttee, and I don't."

"How can she believe in that?" Kumud asked, shocked that someone she loved so dearly would believe in something like self-burning. "Why does Sau Massi worship Satimata?"

Ma answered, "Her husband and his whole family are staunch devotees of the goddess and the ritual."

"Like in the puppet show, Ma?" Kumud's eyes grew big. "Why would people do suttee?"

Ma thought for a moment. "I guess a long time ago it was a kind of an insurance that a wife would take good care of her husband."

"But Sau Massi *does* take good care of her sick husband. Wouldn't she anyway?"

"People didn't seem to think so," Ma said. "And if the person you are married to is not kind to you, you may not want to take good care of him."

"Does Sau Massi believe she can't live by herself after her husband dies?"

"That's what her family thinks. She's started believing them. Maybe they are afraid if he dies she may remarry someone else and thus disgrace her dead husband and them."

"How would that be a disgrace?"

"Listen Kumud, this gets a bit complicated." Ma smoothed Kumud's long hair. "When you are older we'll talk again. You'll know more and understand it better. But Sau Massi sincerely believes in goddess Satimata and the suttee ritual. For now, please don't ask her about it... and don't ask me such questions in front of her."

"Do men believe in suttee?" Kumud asked. "Does Baba believe that?"

"Your father would never believe in something like that!" Ma gasped. "Your father loves you and me."

"If m-m-my husband dies," Kumud stuttered, "do I have to commit suttee?"

"No, *bitiya*!" Ma bellowed. "That is an ancient tradition. You will choose a husband who thinks like Baba. Come here and give me a hug."

Kumud scooted closer to her mother. For the first time, Kumud wondered what else Sau Massi believed in that her parents did not. It was beyond her understanding. All this talk of suttee agitated the wound on her cheek and ear. How could a woman let herself burn alive?

Kumud even wondered if Diwali was not such a beautiful festival after all. Behind the brilliance of a million illuminations was the ever present element of danger. Fire could be used to destroy a life. How could the people you love believe in something like that? And how could Ma and Sau Massi vehemently disagree about such beliefs and yet remain friends?

She shuddered. When she got older, if her husband died, Kumud would never immolate herself. But what if her husband's family forced her to do so? What would she do then?

Sau Massi looked invigorated after her trip to the Satimata temple.

Kumud greeted her hesitantly, searching her face for some sign of disappointment. "How was your temple visit?" she asked.

"Oh, how I wish you were with me," Sau Massi said. "The temple is enormous—five stories high, painted in emerald, pinks and greens. It is made out of marble and yet looks fragile and graceful."

Ma brought a glass of cold water for Sau to drink. "Here, cool down. It is beautiful out but has been unusually hot."

"Yes," Sau agreed. "My throat felt parched the whole day. The floor was cool to the touch after I handed my shoes to the footwear attendant. I drank water from the spigot and splashed it on my face several times."

"What else was there to see?" Kumud was eager to know, but looked at her mother to make sure she was not asking the wrong question.

"There were twelve canopied suttee shrines. And the thirteenth one—the main shrine—was that of Narayani Devi. There is no image of her, just a trident as the symbol of the power of the great goddess." Sau turned to Geeta. "Did you know that pilgrims from all over India and around the world offer extravagant donations to the temple?" Without waiting for an answer she continued. "Their generous donations have transformed Narayani

Satimata's plain mound into an elaborate marble temple and residential complex."

"Didn't your husband donate some money?" Geeta asked.

"Yes. But we are not as prosperous as those expatriated donors," Sau explained. "Their names are etched on marble slabs on the walls of the main temple while my husband's name is carved on a brick laid along the pathway."

Kumud held back a barrage of questions. How could Sau Massi get excited about a ritual like suttee? She also wondered why men didn't commit suttee when their wife dies. But she had promised her mother to keep silent so she zipped her lips together and listened.

"Kumud, go now and prepare your school bag," Ma said suddenly. "Tomorrow is a school day."

Kumud could clearly see the frustration and helplessness in her mother's eyes. Was this why she'd changed the subject? Kumud wasn't sure, but suddenly she too felt worried.

It was still a few days before Sau Massi was to leave, so Kumud reluctantly headed for school. At the end of the day she walked fast toward her home. From a distance she saw someone seated on their front porch. It wasn't her father.

Closer, she noticed a man in traditional garb with a red and yellow *pugdi*, wearing a white kurta and churidar pajama, seated on the cane chair. She guessed him to be a relative of Sau Massi because only a few people in their town dressed in traditional garb like that.

He sprang to his feet and made eye contact.

He was not anyone Kumud recognized. Her pace hastened. "Namaste, Bhaiji," she greeted the stranger politely.

"I'm Sau Ma's stepson. Is Sau Ma not here?"

"She is," Kumud replied. "Did you knock?" She headed for the door and knocked hard. "Is everything okay? Is anything the matter, Bhaiji?"

"My father is very sick," he told her. "They want Sau Ma back home. I've come to take her."

"But she said his health was steady now," Kumud whined. "He was on the mend."

"That's what we thought too, but it turned out to be the calm before the storm."

Ma opened the door and seemed as surprised to see Sau's son as Kumud had been.

Realizing that Sau Massi would leave right away, a pang of pain passed through Kumud's chest. One consoling thought popped into her mind; it was getting dark—almost six o'clock. No bus left that late for a different town. Kumud crossed the fingers on her right hand and covered them with her left as she walked to where everyone was seated.

Sau Massi's stepson gave her the bad news.

Baba and Ma looked dejected but Sau accepted it as God's will. She wasn't emotionally moved but looked restless.

Ma told the stepson that he would have to stay for the night. They could catch the six o'clock bus the next morning.

Dinner was simple and the atmosphere subdued. Kumud did not eat with her usual appetite but she gave an abundant hug to Sau Massi. "I wish you didn't have to go." She felt something different in that moment which she did not understand.

"Me too, *bitiya rani*, my little princess!" Sau's eyes might have glistened more than usual. "Remember you are coming to visit me in a few months! We'll have lots of fun. I will take you to see places you have not visited before. They may not be as lavish as in your fancy town, but they have their charm."

Sau Massi's stepson excused himself and went to bed early.

"You hardly ate anything, Kumud," Ma said. "Are you feeling okay?"

"I'm not hungry."

"Give me an extra farewell hug," Sau Massi asked her. "I don't want you to have to wake up early in the morning."

Kumud hugged and bid namaste to Sau Massi, then she hugged Ma and went to bed.

Once in her room, Kumud could not rid her mind of the puppet stories of suttee, the firewalkers from the mela, and how happy the Satimata temple had made Sau Massi. Slowly she drifted into the world of nightmarish dreams.

Kumud saw herself standing in front of her mother and Sau Massi, watching the firewalkers as they plodded across burning coals. Had they deliberately slowed their speed? Did they want to feel the burn? When they reached the other end of the bed of fire, one of them pointed at Kumud. Were they asking her to join them?

She turned to see what her mother would say. She felt Ma's hands on her shoulders. Sau Massi was not there.

Each firewalker carried a sword in his right hand, something she had not noticed earlier. Many more men joined them to form a circle around the fire pit.

"Where is Sau Massi, Ma?" she asked. But her mother could not hear her.

The men raised their swords and shouted, "Victory to Satimata! Victory to Satimata!" They were now standing shoulder to shoulder around the burning rectangle.

Kumud couldn't see clearly what was happening. The row of men obscured her view of the fire pit. The smell of burning flesh was in the air. She looked up at her mother whose hands were now firm across her shoulders, holding her immobile.

Kumud wanted to help whoever was on that pyre, but her mother's hands gripped her shoulders tight.

Unable to move she cried out, "Someone help!" She was coughing and screaming, "Ma, help her!"

"Kumud, wake up!" She felt her mother patting her arm.

Kumud opened her eyes but the dream had felt so real. She was sweating. She sat up and began to cry.

"Oh my, *bitiya*. You had a nightmare," her mother said holding a glass of water.

"I saw Sau Massi on the bed of burning coal, like the one the firewalkers used." She burst into tears.

"Oh, my heart," said Ma. "Here, drink a little water."

"Did Sau Massi leave?"

"Yes, they left very early. Her son was worried they might miss the bus." Ma brushed the hair out of Kumud's eyes. "You don't want to miss yours either. Go get ready."

Kumud couldn't concentrate in school. She returned brooding, and when she arrived home she found her parents speaking in hushed voices. Ma's eyes were red from crying, and her face was wet from tears.

"What's wrong, Ma?" asked Kumud. "Why are you upset?"

Her parents looked at each other a long moment before Baba spoke. "Sau Massi's husband is very sick," he said. "Your mother is going to go and help her for a few days."

Kumud's breath caught. "Worse than before?"

Ma nodded and paled.

Kumud straightened. She wanted to do something useful. "I want to go too," she said. "I want to help Sau Massi."

Ma sent Baba a worried look. With a tense face she said, "Perhaps it's better if you don't come."

Baba seemed to be considering Ma's words but a glimmer passed his eyes. He said, "Perhaps Kumud is the one who could convince Sau to change her mind. If she sees Kumud, maybe..." His voice trailed off.

Kumud didn't understand what he meant, but the next day she and Ma began the long journey to Sau Massi's house.

They couldn't get tickets for the first bus, but the one after that left at ten o'clock. It was already stifling hot. Then the bus had engine trouble. It finally left the depot at noon when the sun was at its zenith. Once they boarded, Ma let Kumud take the window seat.

Ma was quieter than usual. It made sense. Sau Massi's husband was so sick that he may die. The thought made Kumud sad too. With him being ill, they were not going to have the kind of fun they had during Diwali week.

As Kumud considered what they could do at Sau Massi's home, the bus conductor called for the passengers' attention. They had driven only for an hour but the engine was again misbehaving. They would have to stop at the nearest depot to get it checked. Their arrival time to Neela Nagar would be even later.

People complained and grumbled but couldn't blame the driver. At the bus depot some passengers stepped down, while others remained seated. Ma seemed too distraught to get off the bus. Kumud sensed an urgency in her, and she felt it herself. With each delay, it kept them from reaching Sau in time to help her with her ailing husband.

Kumud tried to speak with her mother, but Ma was so distracted that Kumud gave up. She pulled a book from her bag and began to read.

After the bus was repaired this time, they drove through red chili fields that were ready to be picked.

Under the sunset, the vast fields looked like a painted scenery. Kumud couldn't get enough of it. She nudged her mother, trying to coax her to see how beautiful things looked, but was unable to attract her attention.

When they arrived at Sau Massi's home, Sau was not at the front door to greet them as usual. Instead, men in groups of two or three huddled together talking. Kumud spotted Sau Massi's stepson among them. Then Sau's brother-in-law whispered something in her mother's ear. Ma's face turned white. She gasped and sank to the front step. Holding her arms tightly against her chest, she began to cry and rock herself.

Kumud moved closer. "What's the matter, Ma?" Something awful must have happened because Ma looked more worried than she had the whole day.

Sau Massi's stepson asked if they wanted to step inside to keep his mother company. If Sau would not let them in her room, he said, they could sit in the back room with the other female mourners.

Kumud held her mother's hand as they walked inside. "What did he say to you, Ma?"

"Sau's husband died." Ma's grip tightened as they crossed the porch and passed through a long corridor. They followed the sounds of lamentations to a crowded room. They stood at its threshold where women of different ages were seated on the floor. Some were crying but most were singing. Upon seeing the mother and daughter at the door the women moved closer to the wall, making space near the entry for them to sit.

Ma quietly asked the woman sitting next to them, "Where is Sau?"

"She has shut herself in and does not want to see anyone."

"We have come from Madhya Shahar to meet her. We did not know about the death when we left home. We would like to see her."

The woman nodded and asked a girl to take the two guests to Sau's room.

Sau Massi opened the door when she heard Ma's voice. Her eyes and nose were red. Her expression softened when she saw them. Ma held her in a tight embrace, and they both began to cry.

Sau Massi asked them to sit. Closing the door behind her, she stood solemnly with her palms folded.

"Tell me you're not doing this?" Ma begged.

Sau looked away.

"Are you out of your mind?" Ma, now with tears flowing down her cheeks, separated Sau Massi's palms and held them in her hands.

"Don't cry, Geeta. All is for good," Sau Massi said, patting Ma's head.

On the side table, a lamp lit a framed photograph of her wedding day. In the picture, Sau Massi's head scarf had been removed. Her slender neck and cheekbones were prominently visible. She and her groom, with crow's feet around his eyes, smiled separately. The camera had clearly captured her youth and his age.

"But why, Sau? You can take care of yourself. You can come and stay with me. You have grown sons. There is no reason for you to do this."

"Without my husband I am nothing." Sau Massi sounded indifferent.

Kumud, who was sitting close to her mother and holding her hand, let go and walked next to Sau Massi. "You are very important to me."

Sau kept her hand on Kumud's head and said, "I know, and you are important to me."

Ma raised her voice and repeated what Kumud had said, "But you are very important to both of us, and to Ragu! You are a whole world in yourself! You are the one who taught me about being a woman in my own right. How can you even think about such a thing? What about the pain?"

"His body will be burning too," Sau said as if in a daze.

"But you are alive, Sau. He is dead!" Ma exclaimed.

"Haven't you visited the thirteen shrines of thirteen suttees?" Sau's speech was slow and slurred. "Courageous women become *satis*. I am not a coward."

"Let anyone who calls you a coward go to hell! Don't do this, my sister Sau! How did you become so different? We had similar dreams until we got married."

Ma kept trying to convince Sau Massi that what she was doing was senseless. She kept saying Sau Massi was insane, and helplessly wrung her hands. Kumud could not understand why her mother was so upset because she couldn't believe Sau Massi would commit suttee. She felt embarrassed for Ma because Sau Massi in her finery was doing everything she had been asked to do.

As the sun was about to set, the funeral procession began. Kumud followed with Ma tightly holding her hand. Her mother had wept since they first arrived, which made Kumud cry. Ma's face was pale. Kumud could not fathom that her mother actually believed Sau Massi could do something like suttee.

Ma had pleaded with Sau Massi to reconsider. Mentally tired, Kumud had dozed on and off while the two women talked, though it was mostly Ma speaking because Sau Massi seemed to not be listening to what her mother was saying. In fact, Sau seemed unconscious to this world. When summoned to lead the procession she didn't even say goodbye with her usual affectionate soft kiss.

Several women came. Two held Sau Massi by her arms and led her outside.

Kumud's mother watched awestruck.

"She won't do it," Kumud said tugging on her mother's hand. "Ma, I know she will not do it." When her mother didn't answer, Kumud begged, "Ma, you can't believe she would do it? Do you, Ma?"

Her mother didn't respond but staggered all the way to the place where the procession stopped. Some young men were in charge. The body of Sau Massi's husband was laid on the funeral pyre, a pile of logs on a concrete platform. Some ten feet away from the pile was a designated area where people in the procession were asked to be seated.

Two men led Sau Massi to sit next to her husband. She stumbled all the way there. Then they placed his lifeless head on her lap.

The mourners, friends, neighbors, and some hired criers wept, but Ma didn't seem to have any tears left. She held Kumud close, pressing the child's face into the soft silk of her sari, but Kumud kept turning her head to see what was happening.

A man, with a log lit at one end held it by the other. He stepped closer to the pyre and reached out until the pyre caught the first flame.

Kumud screamed.

Ma pressed her daughter's face into her bosom and tried not to let her see what was happening. But Kumud glimpsed flames multiplying. Smoke rising. Sau Massi screaming. Struggling. Slumping. *Suttee.*

On the bus back home, Kumud sat in a daze. A numbness had overcome her. She could still smell the scent of burning flesh. Sau Massi's cries of agony echoed in her ears. She could taste smoke in her nose, on her tongue.

Shaking, she clung to Ma until her stomach got so twisted that she vomited. Ma caressed her back but had no words to offer. Kumud understood that there was nothing to say, no turmeric paste that could salve the wound they now shared. The sensations she had felt while the suttee was happening replayed over and over again. A shroud of pain seemed to have permanently veiled her inner vision. She now saw everything through a screen of pain.

Kumud wanted to erase the memory, forget what she had seen, but her body wouldn't let go. She'd been changed in ways she didn't yet grasp. Kumud put her forehead against the window and watched the landscape fly by. She didn't recognize it anymore. She didn't recognize herself. She wasn't sure she'd ever see any part of the world the way she had before. The bright red chili fields had lost their beauty. Now they reminded her only of that first flame.

ABOUT THE AUTHOR

The founder of Mindful Writers Groups and Retreats, DR. MADHU BAZAZ WANGU has won awards from Writer's Digest, Feather Quill, Readers Favorite, Next Generation Indie Book, Indie Excellence, and TAZ Awards. She inspires novice as well as advanced creative people to become better writers and creators, and authentic human beings by following the practice of Writing Meditation.

Madhu has written about her own struggle, trials and tribulations as well as pleasurable experiences that have come her way and taught her what it means to feel awe, wonder and afterglow of creative flow. Currently she is writing her tenth book, the fifth fiction, tentatively titled, *Meaning of My Life.*

Dr. Wangu is a regular workshop presenter at writing conferences. She was the Featured Author at Beaver County Book Fest in 2017, Inaugural Guest at International Indo-American Literary Festival, 2020, and that year she won the Pennwriters Meritorious Award. She was the Lunch Keynote Speaker at Pennwriters Annual Conference in 2023.

Visit the website:
MadhuBazazWangu.com

OTHER BOOKS

Fiction

The Last Suttee

The Other Shore

The Immigrant Wife

Chance Meetings

Non-Fiction

Unblock Your Creative Flow

Images of Indian Goddesses

A Goddess is Born

Hinduism

Buddhism

CDs

Mindful Meditation for Writers: Body, Heart, Mind

Mindful Meditation for Writers II: Walking Through the Forest, Awakening the Senses, Mountain and Lotus, Animating Seven Energy Chakra

Meditations for Mindful Writers III: Generosity, Gratitude, Self-Compassion and Trust